The Shiners

A nighttime adventure for children

Kevin Parsons

MAPLE
PUBLISHERS

The Shiners

Author: Kevin Parsons

Text Copyright © Kevin Parsons (2022)

Illustrations Copyright © White Magic Studios

The right of Kevin Parsons to be identified as author of this work has been asserted by the author in accordance with section 77 and 78 of the Copyright, Designs and Patents Act 1988.

First Published in 2022

ISBN: 978-1-915492-11-1 (Paperback)

Book cover design, Illustrations and Book layout by:

White Magic Studios

www.whitemagicstudios.co.uk

Published by:

Maple Publishers

1 Brunel Way,

Slough,

SL1 1FQ, UK

www.maplepublishers.com

A CIP catalogue record for this title is available from the British Library.

One night on planet Earth, somewhere in England .....

Two young children, Harry and his sister Sophie, were both in Harry's room looking out the window and gazing up at the Moon.

It was a big bright ball in the night sky on this clear night and they both began to wonder how this happens and where it goes in the daytime.

Sophie, always the more imaginative and inventive one, said "I know how it happens".

"Ok clever glogs, tell me" said Harry.

"It's simple …. But you couldn't work it out because you're stupid" said Sophie.

"Don't call me stupid. You always think you know everything so just tell me."

"Well, you will just have to wait until tomorrow because I'm tired and I need to go to sleep" replied Sophie and she started to yawn and walk back to her room.

Later that night while Harry and Sophie were both asleep and the Moon was still very big and bright in the night sky……..

Sophie began to dream.

She found herself wandering around on the surface of the Moon.

She tried to look back at planet Earth but it was difficult because it was so bright on the Moon and she needed to shield her eyes with her hands. Just as she squinted a look at planet Earth she felt a tap on her right shoulder that made her jump …..

Then, as she turned around she could see a figure. Just a bit taller than herself, wearing dark glasses and holding a book of some kind.

She was just about to run away when she realized it was….

Her brother Harry!

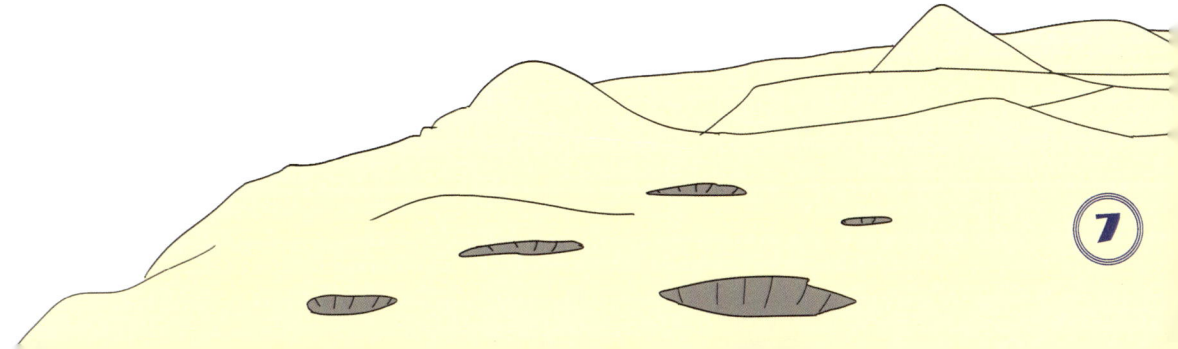

.... "Whoa.... What are you doing here and how did you get here and what's the book in your hand... and ....and...." Sophie was talking very fast.

"Heyyyy, so many questions" said Harry. Then......." It's a dream silly, so I got here the same way as you did... by magic."

"Anyway, you will need these" said Harry as he handed Sophie an extra pair of dark glasses to put on.

"Oh, thanks Harry. This is much better now I can see without squinting in this light. Sunglasses make all the difference."

"They're not sunglasses, they're MOONGLASSES and I knew you would need them here ... so now who's the stupid one eh" said Harry.

"OK, sorry, replied Sophie, then ... "what's that book you have with you?"

"Ah... we are going to need this soon, because I figured out how the Moon works, and you didn't think I could".

LUNAR TO ENGLISH

"So, you know about the 'Moonies'?" asked Sophie.

"Moonies? ... I think you mean the 'Shiners' said Harry. "But anyway ... I think we both know they control the Moonshine, so I guess we are both right ".

Then Sophie pointed to the book asking Harry to explain what it's about.

"Well" said Harry... "When we get to meet the Shiners, I'm pretty sure you will find this book useful as it's a Lunar to English translation book. Because I figured out the Shiners probably don't speak English".

"What's 'Lunar'?" asked Sophie.

"Lunar is Moonspeak" replied Harry, feeling very smart.

"Ok, that's great Harry, now let's go find the Moonies, or Shiners. I think they have a control area over in that shallow crater thing over there. "....

The adventure begins .....

So Harry and Sophie started to run excitedly over to the crater. They got up to the top edge to look over and then Sophie shouted "wow, look Harry, there's some Shiners over the other side and they look like they're glowing in a bright green colour".

As Harry rushed up to the edge to get a good view, he slipped over and rolled down the side into the crater and was shouting in panic to Sophie.

"It's ok Harry, I'm right behind you" said Sophie.

At this point some of the Shiners heard them and began to hurry towards Harry and Sophie and, as they came closer, they could hear the Shiners talking a strange language.

"Oh dear" said Sophie ... "I can't understand what they're saying, so we may need that book of yours Harry ".

As Harry tried to search for a word or two to try and communicate, Sophie was suddenly surprised to hear one of the Shiners say "Hello, my name is Pongo, who are you? "

"Oh, you speak English" said a relieved Sophie.

"Of course we do. This is a dream, isn't it? So we can speak any language."

"That's good" said Harry, getting to his feet …. "So I don't need this book anymore" and dropped it down into the moon dust.

"Well, I'm Harry and this is Sophie ".

"Hee hee, what silly names you both have. Anyway, come and meet my friends and we can show you around" said Pongo.

As they walked over to meet the others Pongo asked "What's all that stuff on your heads?"

"Oh, it's hair" said Harry.

"Why is Sophie's hair longer than yours Harry"?

"She's a girl" said Harry.

"Aren't you a girl?" asked Pongo.

"No, he's a boy" came the quick reply from Sophie.

"What's the difference?" asked a confused Pongo.

"Oh …. It's …. "Complicated" said Sophie interrupting Harry, then … "Let's get over to your friends Pongo "

And off they went…

As they approached the Shiners, Pongo spoke to them first in Moonspeak. He pointed to Harry and Sophie, then said in English "Come and say hello to everyone ".

"This is Gonk, he helps keep the control area clean and tidy. "

"Hello Harry and Sophie" said Gonk.

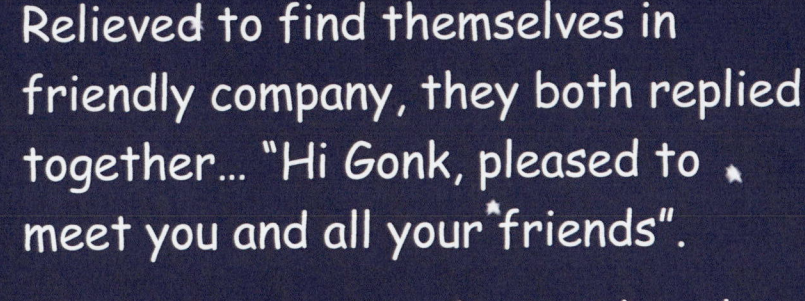

Relieved to find themselves in friendly company, they both replied together... "Hi Gonk, pleased to meet you and all your friends".

Then they were both introduced to all the others .... There are only six in total anyway.

The other four are .... Klik and Klak, they operate the big switch to turn the Moon on and off when needed. Then finally there is Deek and Jingle .... It's their job to keep a look out at the top of the crater for Sunrise ...

This is the signal to switch the Moon off.

"My job" said Pongo, "is to keep things in order around here, so I simply oversee each job in a way."

Harry and Sophie seemed very impressed by all this and had noticed that the Shiners were excited to have them as visitors.

Gonk said "What's it like living on Planet Earth? We are always looking over at it when we switch the Moonshine on."

"Oh, it's ok" said Harry.

"More fun here" said Sophie, adding... "it's much brighter."

"Oh, wait until we switch the moonshine off at sunrise. It's dark then and we can all rest or sleep" said Jingle.

"So, do you switch it on at Sundown?" asked Sophie.

"Yes, that's exactly right." said Deek.

"And you can go with us up to the top soon when we will be looking to give the signal to switch off at sunrise "said Jingle.

"That sounds fun" said Harry.

Sophie was getting excited too, then suddenly thought... "if you all sleep at sunrise when it's dark here with the moonshine turned off, how does Jingle and Deek know when to wake up to check the Sundown? "

Then Pongo said "I have to be alert at all times and I make sure to give them a nudge in plenty of time for them to get in position at the top of the crater over there."

"Got it!" replied Harry and Sophie together.

Then Pongo needed to remind them to remove their moonglasses when the moonshine is turned off at sunrise ....

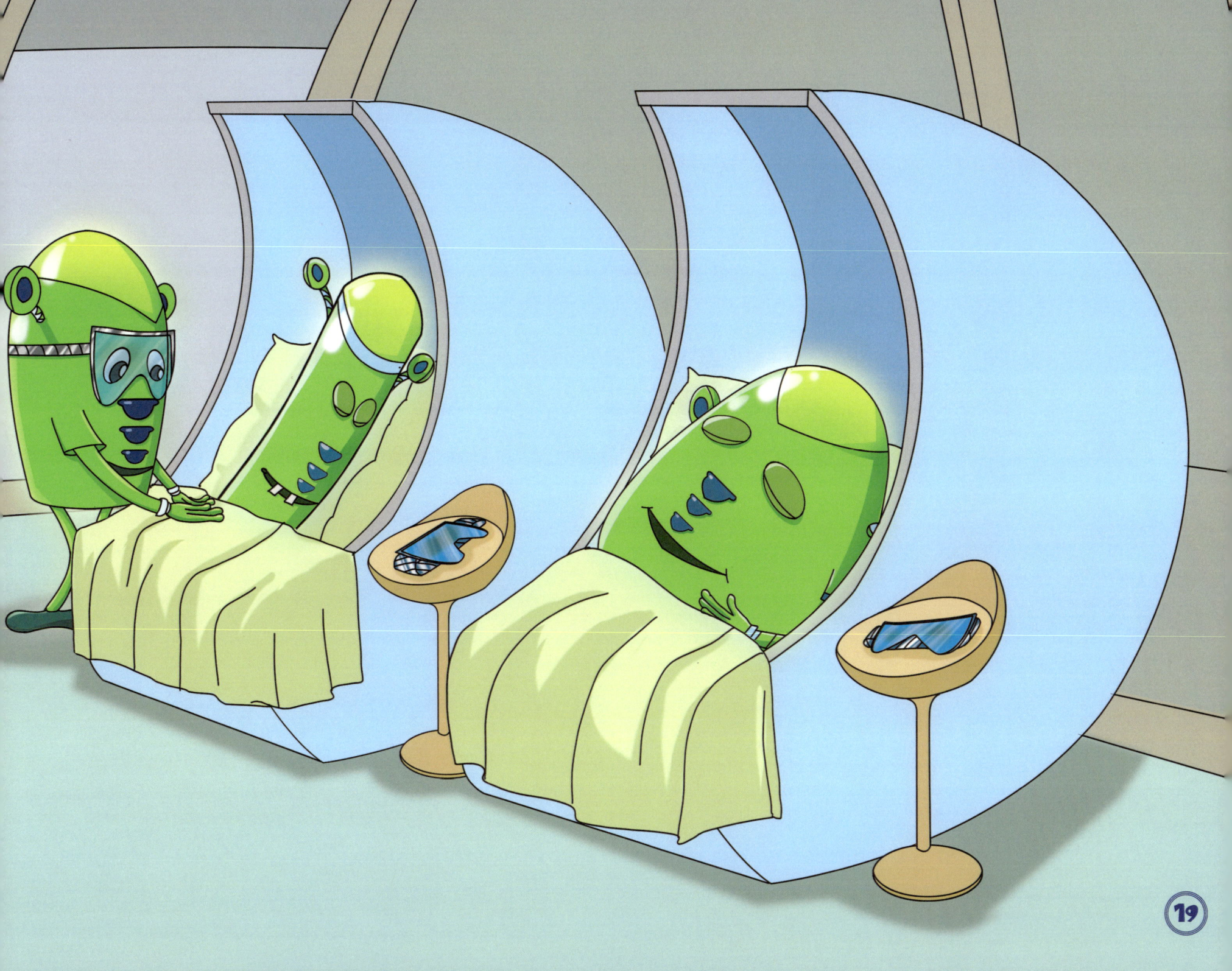

"Ah, yes" they both replied, and began to laugh thinking how silly it would be in the dark with moonglasses on.

Later, Harry and Sophie were talking with Klik and Klak as they were observing how the switch is operated to turn the moonshine on and off, when suddenly Pongo shouted ....."Deek, Jingle ... you both need to make your way to the top and check for the sunrise , I think it's nearly time."

"OK" they replied and began to run to get in position to watch the sunrise. Then Klik and Klak told Harry and Sophie to move to the side so they could both be ready too.

"This is exciting" said Sophie, and Harry was looking up to the ridge to see if Jingle and Deek were signalling.

Then everyone heard Jingle shout to Deek... "Sun's coming up now, Deek" so Deek started jumping up and down waving his arms and shouting "OK, now!!!"

This was the signal for Klik and Klak as they pushed the big switch over to turn the moonshine off, then ....

It was dark!!!

"Moonglasses off" shouted Pongo, then to Harry and Sophie he said "you both look as tired as I feel so we should get some sleep and rest now."

As Harry and Sophie began to fall asleep, comfortable and warm, they suddenly both heard a knock on their doors and the voice of their Dad shouting "wake up you two,

The breakfast is nearly ready and time to get ready for school"

Then, just as he walked back to the kitchen, Dad heard a knock on the front door.

When he opened it he was very surprised to find a strange looking small figure glowing a luminous green colour standing there.

"Hello, my name is Pongo, please could you give this to Harry and Sophie …. I think they left it behind when they came to visit us", and handed Dad a book.

When Dad looked up Pongo had disappeared in a flash of light. Leaving Dad very puzzled.

At breakfast , Dad walked up to the table keeping the book behind his back and asked Harry and Sophie if they have anything they needed to tell him ?

"No" came their reply .

"So who is Pongo?" asked Dad.

Sophie and Harry looked shocked and said "Wow! You must have had the same dream we had last night Dad."

"Dream??" asked Dad...

Then dropped the book on the table and they all read the title...

"Lunar to English Translation"

Watch out for the next book in the series:

THE SHINERS – PART 2

GONKS SECRET

Lightning Source UK Ltd.
Milton Keynes UK
UKRC031010070922
408472UK00001B/11